Beth and the Bugs

Level 2D

Written by Sam Hay
Illustrated by Ann Johns
Reading Consultant: Betty Franchi

About Phonics

Spoken English uses more than 40 speech sounds. Each sound is called a *phoneme*. Some phonemes relate to a single letter (d–o–g) and others to combinations of letters (sh–ar–p). When a phoneme is written down, it is called a *grapheme*. Teaching these sounds, matching them to their written form, and sounding out words for reading is the basis of phonics.

Early phonics instruction gives children the tools to sound out, blend, and say the words without having to rely on memory or guesswork. This instruction gives children the confidence and ability to read unfamiliar words, helping them progress toward independent reading.

About the Consultant

Betty Franchi is an American educator with a Bachelor's Degree in Elementary and Middle Education as well as a Master's Degree in Special Education. Betty holds a National Boards for Professional Teaching Standards certification. Throughout her 24 years as a teacher, she has studied and developed an expertise in Phonetic Awareness and has implemented phonetic strategies, teaching many young children to read, including students with special needs.

Reading tips

This book focuses on the *th* sound.

Tricky and/or new words in this book

Any words in bold may have unusual spellings or are new and have not yet been introduced.

Tricky and/or new words in this book

the I said my
her they good

Extra ways to have fun with this book

After the readers have finished the story, ask them questions about what they have just read.

What bugs does Beth find in her bag?
What did Dot spot in the mud?

Explain that the two letters *th* make one sound. Think of other words that use the *th* sound, such as *thanks* and *then*.

A Pronunciation Guide

This grid highlights the sounds used in the story and offers a guide on how to say them.

s as in sat	a as in ant	t as in tin	p as in pig	i as in ink
n as in net	c as in cat	e as in egg	h as in hen	r as in rat
m as in mug	d as in dog	g as in get	o as in ox	u as in up
l as in log	f as in fan	b as in bag	j as in jug	v as in van
w as in wet	z as in zip	y as in yet	k as in kit	qu as in quick
x as in box	ff as in off	ll as in ball	ss as in kiss	zz as in buzz
ck as in duck	pp as in puppy	nn as in bunny	rr as in arrow	gg as in egg
dd as in daddy	bb as in chubby	tt as in attic	sh as in shop	ch as in chip
th as in them	th as in thin			

Be careful not to add an /uh/ sound to /s/, /t/, /p/, /c/, /h/, /r/, /m/, /d/, /g/, /l/, /f/ and /b/. For example, say /ff/ not /fuh/ and /sss/ not /suh/.

Beth is with **her** class.
They go on a bus to find bugs.

They run up **the** path.

"**I** spot a thick slug in the mud!" **said** Dot.

“I spot a red moth on that log!”
said Nat.
“I spot a thin bug!” said Tom.

Beth is sad. “I did not spot a bug,” said Beth.

"I cannot check **my** bug list."

"Picnic?" asks Miss Hill.

"Yum!" said Beth.
The kids sit on a big log.

Beth gets a bun from her bag.

But Beth has a shock!

“Bugs!” yells Beth.

Beth and the other kids spot
a lot of bugs in the bag.

Thud! The bag fell. “Ants,” said Miss Hill.

"**Good** job, Beth!"

Beth can check her bug list.

But Beth has lost her bun!

OVER 48 TITLES IN SIX LEVELS
Betty Franchi recommends...

Some titles from Level 1

978 1 84898 747 0

978 1 84898 750 0

978 1 84898 752 4

978 1 84898 751 7

Other titles to enjoy from Level 2

978 1 84898 756 2

978 1 84898 759 3

978 1 84898 762 3

Some titles from Level 3

978 1 84898 768 5

978 1 84898 764 7

978 1 84898 765 4

978 1 84898 767 8

An Hachette Company
First Published in the United States by TickTock, an imprint of Octopus Publishing Group.
www.octopusbooksusa.com

Distributed in the US by
Hachette Book Group USA
237 Park Avenue, New York NY 10017, USA

Distributed in Canada by
Canadian Manda Group
165 Dufferin Street, Toronto, Ontario, Canada M6K 3H6

ISBN 978 1 84898 758 6

Printed and bound in China
10 9 8 7 6 5 4 3 2 1